Edward Lear KING OF NONSENSE

Edward Lear

KING OF NONSENSE

A biography by
GLORIA KAMEN

illustrated by

Edward Lear and Gloria Kamen

ATHENEUM · 1990 · NEW YORK

To Julie, Ruth, and Tina

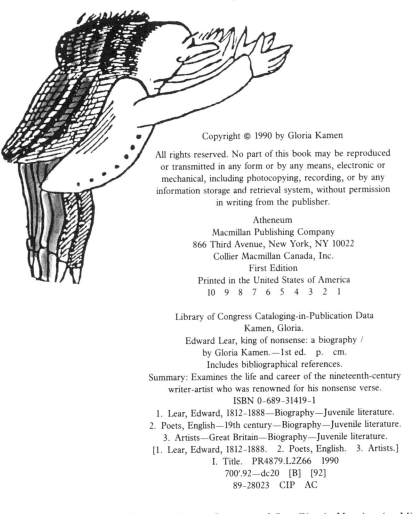

Atheneum
Macmillan Publishing Company
866 Third Avenue, New York, NY 10022
Collier Macmillan Canada, Inc.
First Edition
Printed in the United States of America
10 9 8 7 6 5 4 3 2 1

Library of Congress Cataloging-in-Publication Data
Kamen, Gloria.
Edward Lear, king of nonsense: a biography /
by Gloria Kamen.—1st ed. p. cm.
Includes bibliographical references.
Summary: Examines the life and career of the nineteenth-century writer-artist who was renowned for his nonsense verse.
ISBN 0-689-31419-1
1. Lear, Edward, 1812–1888—Biography—Juvenile literature.
2. Poets, English—19th century—Biography—Juvenile literature.
3. Artists—Great Britain—Biography—Juvenile literature.
[1. Lear, Edward, 1812–1888. 2. Poets, English. 3. Artists.]
I. Title. PR4879.L2Z66 1990
700′.92—dc20   [B] [92]
89-28023 CIP AC

Joseph Turner's *Venice: Dogana and San Giorgio Maggiore* (p. 14), Widener Collection 1942, and Edward Lear's *View of Ceriana* (p. 53), Ailsa Mellon Bruce Fund, both courtesy of the National Gallery of Art, Washington.

CONTENTS

Books written and illustrated by Gloria Kamen
Fiorello
Charlie Chaplin
Kipling
The Ringdoves
"Paddle," Said the Swan

Edward Lear KING OF NONSENSE

1. Lear and Foss

Foss, a untin.

The sun did not reach the studio window facing north but the terrace and garden were warm. Even in winter Italy was usually sunny and pleasant. It was for this reason most of all that Edward Lear left cold and rainy England, his home. It was asthma, cursed asthma leaving him gasping for breath, that made him an exile from his own land!

Lear sat before his easel carefully filling in the details of a large landscape painting, his cat, Foss, asleep at his feet. Foss was getting old. How long ago, Lear wondered, had he written these lines:

> *'O lovely Pussy! O Pussy, my love,*
> *What a beautiful Pussy you are,*
> *You are,*
> *You are,*
> *What a beautiful Pussy you are!'*

Foss

It was in a poem in his second book of nonsense songs and poems, of course, written just after a shaggy kitten adopted him as his master. Almost immediately after it was published children began memorizing "The Owl and the Pussy-cat" and made the poem one of their favorites. And, to his surprise, Edward Lear the landscape painter became known throughout Britain as *Mr. Nonsense*. Not only was he not offended by the title but he rather enjoyed his newfound fame.

"I like to think," wrote Lear to a friend, "that if a man ain't able to do any great service to his fellow critters, it is better (than nothing) to make half a million children laugh innocently."

Childhood, as Lear knew from his own, is not always a happy time.

Edward Lear was the twentieth child in a family of twenty-one children. There had been thirteen girls and six boys before him. There were three *Sarahs* (two died as infants), three *Henrys* and two *Catherines* in a row. Only by chance did he survive, for he was a delicate and sickly baby.

When Edward was born, the Lear family was a happy, prosperous one. As the family grew so did the number of servants. At one point father Jeremiah Lear, a successful stockbroker, bought twelve horses and carriages to take his large family on Sunday outings. The caravan of carriages formed a lively parade down the city streets during the early 1800s, years before those same streets heard the *put, put, put* of an automobile. Their comfortable house, called Bowman's Lodge, sat atop a steep hill overlooking the city of London.

But their pleasant life ended suddenly when their father's business ventures failed and left him in serious debt. This unexpected tragedy resulted in the loss of their home, servants, and way of life. Jeremiah Lear was sent to the King's Bench Debtor's Prison, leaving the family penniless. The oldest sisters were forced to find work as domestic servants. The family was separated, never to be together again. The year was 1825.

In the early nineteenth century, very few women worked by choice outside the home. Widows, unmarried women with no one to support them, and the young daughters of poor families were forced to support themselves. Edward's sisters had expected to marry and live comfortably in a large house with servants. They were totally unprepared for the hard work and long hours of servant girls. Three of Edward's sisters, hired out to rich families, died within the first year after their father was sent to prison. Only Ann, the eldest, was spared this punishing life because of a small allowance left to her by her grandmother. With this tiny income Ann moved into her own flat, taking thirteen-year-old Edward with her.

There was an Old Man of the East,
Who gave all his children a feast;
　　But they all ate so much,
　　And their conduct was such,
That it killed that Old Man of the East.

Sister Ann

Bowman's Lodge

2. Ann, Sister and Mother

Ann was the name of both Edward's sister and mother, but for him, his sister was more truly his mother. From the time he was born, his eldest sister watched over him, for by then his mother no longer took an interest in her babies, so many of them having died in the first few years of their lives.

At the age of twenty-four, when she should have married and had children of her own, his sister chose to devote herself to his care instead. Ann, though not especially pretty, was well educated and born with a sweet and gentle nature. Twice she had refused offers of marriage, possibly fearing that she, like her mother, would be overburdened with child-bearing. Besides, it was clear from the time he was very little that Edward needed all her care.

When only five years old, Edward began to have "fits" or "spells"—sometimes as many as three or four a day. Neither the family nor

Edward talked about them to others, for in the 1800s it was best to keep such things secret. If, as Ann suspected, it was the "falling sickness," as epilepsy was called, there was nothing that could be done for it. There were no medicines or treatment, for little was known or understood about this disease. Those with epilepsy were often thought to be "possessed of demons," or insane, and were hidden away in asylums or hospitals for life. Today, because of a better understanding of the causes of this disease, epileptics, with the aid of special medication, are able to lead normal lives.

Edward's fits were usually mild and ended quickly. From childhood on he knew the warning signs and would go to his room, out of sight, until a seizure was over. He did this for the rest of his life, so that even good friends who saw him regularly did not know of his illness. He was only seven when he first had what he called "the Morbids," fits of depression much deeper than just feeling unhappy. These mood changes and his restlessness could also have been due to the epilepsy.

Because of his "fits" and frequent attacks of asthma, Ann began tutoring her brother at home instead of sending him to school. While they still lived at Bowman's Lodge, and with several older sisters to help, Lear was taught the basic skills of reading, arithmetic, and writing. His sister Sarah, who had had some art training, noticed Edward's unusual ability to draw and started giving him art lessons. She saw this talent as a way for Edward to earn his living later on, for there were few opportunities in England at that time for boys with no money and little schooling.

Most of what Lear was taught to draw— flowers, birds, and butterflies—were subjects usually left for young ladies and maiden aunts, subjects he might not have chosen himself. But he did them well, for he was eager to please his loving and devoted sisters.

When, at age eleven, he was sent to school for the first time, he was no better or worse than the other students. Formal schooling, he later believed, might have crushed his originality. Perhaps this was a way of looking at the bright side of being deprived of early boyhood friendships. Except for his brothers and sisters, Lear had had few playmates while growing up. He spent much of his time alone drawing or reading poetry.

One of his earliest attempts at poetry was something he wrote when he was fourteen for his sister Ann's birthday, a rhyme one hundred lines long, each line ending with the suffix "ation." It begins seriously enough with the lines:

Dear, and very dear relation,
Time who flies without cessation....

but, by the middle of the verse, Lear was already creating new words and taking liberties with the English language with words like *deplumation*, *deliquation*, *obtrectation*, and *refulerlation*.

In 1827, the year after his fourteenth birthday, a tall and lanky Lear was sent out into the world "without a farthing to his name" to earn his living, for in nineteenth century England childhood was shortened by many years. Children as young as ten and eleven were sent to work in shops and factories.

Lear was fortunate to have had special training in art, which helped him find a job in an art studio instead of becoming a clerk or factory worker. In addition to his studio job, doing "uncommon queer shop sketches, coloring prints, screens, and fans," he made "morbid disease drawings for hospitals and certain doctors." Before the use of color photography, doctors relied on artist's drawings to show examples of diseased tissues or abnormal growths in the human body. It didn't take great artistic skill or originality to color prints or fans, but Lear was learning to use paints and brushes skillfully. The medical drawings were more demanding. They required great accuracy and an eye for detail, but the subject matter—copying tumors, rashes, or deformities—was not something he enjoyed.

Lear's real love was drawing from nature. This enjoyment grew each time he visited his married sister, Sarah, who lived in the Sussex countryside, where he spent many pleasant weekends exploring the fields and woods surrounding the village. It was a welcome change from the cramped London flat he then shared with Ann.

Not far from Sarah lived the wealthy earl of Egremont, whose private collection of English landscape paintings was one of the best in the country. It was there that Lear first saw the paintings of J. M. W. Turner, England's most outstanding landscape artist. Seeing for the first time the beauty that could be achieved by a master landscape artist, Lear was deter-

Venice: Dogana & San Giorgio Maggiore by *J. M. W. Turner*

mined to become a more serious artist himself.

His first step was to escape from doing "morbid disease drawings" by finding a job with a Mr. Prideaux Selby, who was working on a series of bird prints. Selby could not have made a better choice of apprentice. Lear was eager, hard working, and a quick learner. With Selby's help, Lear learned how to transfer his drawings onto a lithographic stone, the method used to print the finished pictures. Each of the lithographs, printed with black ink, was colored by hand and then sold to collectors. There was a new popular interest in owning bird prints, particularly those of birds that had never been seen in Britain. It was the time of British explorations to lands all over the globe. Charles Darwin had returned from a five-year voyage around the world, during which he collected rare species of plant and animal life and startled the world with his new scientific theory of evolution. Some years later, a series of prints of Darwin's collection of rare animals was being prepared for publication. Young Edward Lear, now an assistant to another famous printmaker named John Gould, made several of these prints, to which Gould signed his own name.

Other naturalists and explorers returned from Asia, Africa, and the Americas with new collections of exotic birds, some alive, others skinned and stuffed. Such rare specimens were greatly prized.

One of those who kept a collection of unusual *live* animals on his large estate was Lord Stanley, who was president and supporter of the newly organized London Zoo. It was at the zoo that Edward Lear's life as an artist took a giant step foward.

There was an old person of Nice,
Whose associates were usually Geese.
     They walked out together,
          In all sorts of weather,
That affable person of Nice!

Edward, 13th Earl of Derby

The Runcible Bi

3. Parrots, Painters, and Lords

Now that Lear knew the art of bird illustrating, he decided to do a series on his own. It was an ambitious project for an eighteen year old— to do twelve sets of prints of all the parrots then known to man. This time the prints would carry *his* name. He chose the parrot family *Psittacidae* (the scientific, Latin name), because of the bird's dramatic coloring. So, feeling confident enough to ask permission to sketch the parrots at the Regent's Park Zoo in London, he set to work.

His intention was to draw the birds from life instead of working from the dead skins and stuffed specimens he'd used in Selby's studio. In order to draw each of them as accurately as possible, Lear had the animal keeper hold the sometimes angry, hostile bird while he measured beak, claw, tail, and wingspread. Whenever possible, he wanted to do his drawings life-size, or, if a particular bird was very

large, to scale it down just enough to fit the pages of his portfolio. The idea was novel; the results were unusually successful. His finished prints were considered as good as any by the best-known bird artists of his day, including the American naturalist John James Audubon.

While working on this series of prints in the rooms shared with his sister, Lear warned a friend who planned to visit them that every chair except one was filled with pages from his portfolio. "For the last twelve months," wrote Lear, "I have so moved—thought—looked at—and existed among parrots that should any transmigration take place at my decease [in other words, should he reappear in some other form after death], I am sure…it would be as one of the Psittacidae [a parrot]."

Lear spent the year between his nine-teenth and twentieth birthdays completing his portfolio of parrots, paying for the cost of printing out of his own pocket, though he was earning no money at the time. But his costly gamble succeeded beyond all expectations. The lifelike appearance of his birds caught the attention of many collectors, including Lord Stanley, who greatly admired the young artist's work.

Finding Lear sketching in Regent's Park Zoo one day, Lord Stanley introduced himself. Lear was asked if he would be interested in making a set of drawings of Lord Stanley's collection of unusual animals for a book he wished to publish. The collection, housed on the Stanley estate at Knowsley Hall, outside Liverpool, was one of the most famous menageries in Europe. It included a short-toed eagle, a civet, a tree rat, a red-billed toucan, and something called a yagouarondi from tropical America, an animal resembling a wildcat.

Twenty-year-old Edward Lear readily accepted the offer and moved into Knowsley Hall, where he was housed, along with other employees, in the part of the manor house reserved for servants.

Among the members of the family living at Knowsley was the twelfth earl of Derby, father of Lord Stanley. This warmhearted eighty-year-old gentleman enjoyed the company of his numerous family and friends. On any given day, the dinner table at Knowsley would be filled with as many as forty to one hundred guests. Many of them were the children, grandchildren, and great-grandchildren of the old earl. Many of these same children became Lear's lifelong friends.

Besides the extended family of the earl, there were gardeners, gamekeepers, chamber-maids, and butlers on the estate. The perma-nent staff also included the nursemaids and governesses who took care of the children. Among this collection of lords, ladies, and very proper adults, Lear felt awkward and confined, wishing at times he could "giggle heartily and hop on one leg down the great gallery [hall]." Except when he was with the younger children, Lear was conscious of his ungainly looks and ill-fitting clothes. More and more Lear took to spending his spare time in the nursery entertaining the children, who began to look forward to his visits. To amuse them he would take some paper and, with a few quick strokes, caricature the animals he had been drawing during the day. At the same time he recited and wrote nonsense verses to go with them.

Like other members of the staff, Lear took his meals downstairs in the stewards' room when he first arrived. But Lord Stanley noticed before long that the children were begging to be excused from the dinner table as soon as they finished eating and would head straight for the stewards' room. The attraction, it became clear, was Mr. Lear. Discovering this, Lord Stanley invited his artist/naturalist to join them upstairs at the family dinner table, to find out what it was about Lear that so appealed to the children. It was soon after this that Lear became a special guest of the family, charming the adults with his gentle wit and imagination as he had the children.

Lear remained at Knowsley Hall for most of the next five years, some of his most rewarding, for it was there that he discovered his love for creating nonsense for children.

Before he left the Stanley estate, Lear had made up enough drawings and limericks to fill two small volumes. But he had no thought of showing them to anyone beside the children at Knowsley, for he was intent, at age twenty-five, on making his reputation as a fine nature artist—and with good reason. His one hundred studies, printed in a book about Lord Stanley's menagerie, were of the same fine quality as his bird prints.

Working in painstaking detail on his set of animal prints for so many years, it had been a relief and a release to dash off lively pen caricatures for the children. And it seems clear why the children loved them so. His words and pictures had only one purpose: to make them laugh. In the 1830s this was indeed rare. Most of the books made for children were designed to teach them lessons or morals. A boy who ate too many cookies would not only get *fat*, he might *explode* and never be seen again! "Bad" children were warned about the punishment to expect for being naughty, selfish, or careless. The illustrations were either frightening or dull. No wonder the Stanley children welcomed everything Lear wrote.

During his years at the old thirteenth-

Woodcut for Little Red Riding Hood used in France and England in 1729 and 1802

century Stanley estate, Lear created an audience eager to hear more of his brand of humor, his play with words. They were ready to laugh at his misspellings of common words, his run-on phrases and made-up names. In his letters it was not unusual for him to call himself a *nartist* who drew *pigchers* from his *ozbervations* or that he rode *grumpy roargroany* camels over *rumby-tumby* ravines and *jizzdoodle* rocks. It was Lear's own imaginative, made-up, "Learical" language.

25

Very likely Lear started composing his comic rhymes at Knowsley after finding and reading the book *Anecdotes and Adventures of Fifteen Gentlemen*, published in 1822 or 1823. It contained the following verse:

There was a sick man of Tobago
Liv'd long on rice-gruel and sago;
But at last, to his bliss,
The physician said this—
To a roast leg of mutton you may go.

This same rhythmic form was used in the verses Lear wrote for children. A flood of several hundred of them bounced out of

Old Man of Coblenz

Lear's fertile imagination in the next twenty-five years.

Lear's rhymes were not called limericks until years later. One reason given for the name was that Lear's verses resembled the popular form of rhyming in County Limerick, Ireland.

In a typical limerick each rhyme starts with the words *There was*, adding...*an old man, or lady, or a young person*, and is four or five lines long, depending on how it is set on the page. The last line is a variation of the first one, as in this one by Lear:

> *There was an Old Man of Coblenz,*
> *The length of whose legs was immense;*
> *He went with one prance,*
> *From Turkey to France,*
> *That surprising Old Man of Coblenz.*

Here is another he wrote:

> *There was a Young Lady of Troy,*
> *Whom several large flies did annoy;*
> *Some she killed with a thump,*
> *Some she drowned at the pump,*
> *And some she took with her to Troy*

In 1837 Lear's set of animal prints for Lord Stanley was completed despite Lear's increasing trouble with poor eyesight. "I can no longer draw any bird smaller than an ostrich," he wrote. Unable to see the fine markings in bird feathers or patterns in animal skins, he abandoned the art he had done for so many years. In June of 1837, he left Knowsley for a trip through Europe to become a landscape painter, arriving in Italy with a pocket of sketches made along the way.

There was an Old Man who said, 'Hush!
I perceive a young bird in this bush!'
    When they said—'is it small?'
    He replied—'Not at all!
It is four times as big as this bush!'

4. The Wanderer

Though poor eyesight made Lear give up drawing birds and animals, being a landscape painter suited him. He liked to wander and explore new places, often walking as much as fifteen to twenty miles a day. His health soon started to improve in the milder, drier climate of southern Europe. He no longer suffered from as many bouts of asthma, and as for his "fits," it hardly mattered where he lived. During the hot summer months, Lear left his home in Rome to sketch in other parts of Italy, returning with studies he used for landscape paintings and prints. He returned to Britain only occasionally to exhibit his work and to visit Ann and his friends.

When Lear first arrived in Rome, Italy, the city was filled with other British tourists and artists. A sketch of Lear made by an artist friend shows him at age twenty-five wearing a thin mustache and a pair of round eyeglasses on a somewhat prominent nose. He is dressed in a soft shirt and vest. It is not at all the face of an ugly man, as he often described himself. What can be seen is the gentle expression in the eyes and mouth, not yet hidden by the huge beard, "big enough for birds to make their nest in," that he wore in later years.

Lear was unhappy that he could not persuade his sister Ann to come live in Italy. He wrote to her faithfully, as before; his letters became a running diary of all he did and saw. Included in some of his letters were thumbnail sketches of places he visited.

It was in letters to his friends, though, that Lear used puns, nonsensical stories, and caricatures to charm them the way he had the Stanleys. One of these friends was a nobleman named Chichester Fortesque, whom he met while Fortesque was on a tour of Europe.

"Delightful companion, full of nonsense, puns, riddles, everything in the shape of fun," said Fortesque. "I don't know when I have met anyone to whom I took so great a liking." Fortesque was twenty-two; Lear, eleven years older, but in spirit Lear seemed the younger of the two.

In his numerous letters to *40scue* (the way Lear sometimes wrote Fortesque's name), Lear freely translated English spelling to "Learical" spelling, knowing it would amuse his friend. He wrote about having a *nemptystummuk* when he was hungry, and of eating *brefiss* to fill it in the hotel *coughy room*. He told his friend all about his art *eggsibishun* and that his *landskips* were selling very well.

Their hundreds of letters, written over Lear's lifetime, continued to show the great affection they shared even when they rarely met. Fortesque later became an important member of the British government, whose duties left him little time for travel. And Lear's visits to Britain became less frequent when sketching expeditions to distant lands lasted for months. His *fizzicle* condition worsened, especially after one of these tiring trips. Sometimes, he wrote, he had *phits of coffin* that kept him in bed.

As often happened, Lear received many

more invitations to dinner than he could or even wanted to attend. Having to say no, politely and graciously, was a constant chore. Here, for example, is one way he apologized to his host for not being able to come to dinner when he had a bad cold. With it was a cartoon showing him in the condition described below:

I have sent for 2 large tablecloths to blow my nose on, having already used up all my handkerchiefs. And altogether I am so unfit for company that I propose getting into a bag and being hung up to a bough of a tree till this tyranny is overpast....

Yours sincerely,
Edward Lear

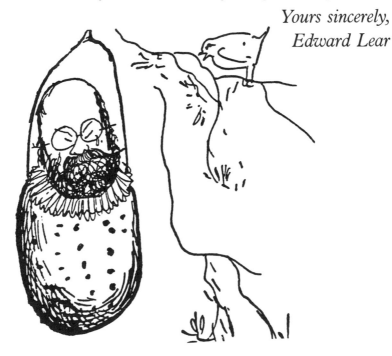

Italy became Lear's home for the next eight years but his heart remained in Britain, where his friends and sisters lived. Then, in 1845, for one last time, he tried to move back to his native country, bringing with him the materials for his new travel book of landscapes in and around Rome. To his great surprise, his book was the reason for a most unusual invitation and honor from Queen Victoria of England.

The Zigzag Zealous Zebra
who carried five Monkeys on his back
all the way to Jellibolee.

Queen
Victoria

5. Her Majesty, Queen Victoria

At twenty-seven, Queen Victoria was the ruler of a vast empire that stretched across many oceans. It included parts of Southeast Asia and colonies in Africa and the Middle East.

In the summer of 1846, a request to Edward Lear arrived from Queen Victoria. She had been very impressed by his book of drawings of Rome and its environs and suggested to Lear that he give her twelve drawing lessons. This request would have made any artist in the British Empire proud, as it no doubt made Lear. It *also* would have made *most* artists seek advice on how to behave and dress for a meeting with the queen. Not so with Edward Lear, who arrived at Queen Victoria's stately country home dressed in his usual careless fashion. The gatekeeper, thinking him some sort of madman, motioned him away. It took some effort to prove his identity—that he was, indeed, the new art tutor—before Lear was admitted through the gate.

To add to his mistakes, Lear either forgot or was unaware of the proper way to address his queen, often omitting the words "Your Majesty" when speaking to her. It was an embarrassment to others in the room even when the queen graciously pretended not to notice. During yet another visit to the palace, when the queen showed Lear her collection of beautiful miniature paintings, he blurted out: "Oh! Where did you get all these beautiful things?" To which the queen quietly replied, "I inherited them, Mr. Lear." (Imagine an American visitor to the White House asking the president of the United States how he happened to be living in such a beautifully furnished house!) Lear fulfilled his duty as art tutor to the queen, but his natural modesty was far from overwhelmed by this honor.

Although he was already recognized as an artist with talent, particularly in drawing animals and landscapes, Lear felt he needed more formal art training. He particularly wanted to improve his drawing of the human figure and to learn more about oil painting. So, at the age of thirty-seven, Lear applied to the

Royal Academy (Art) School of London for admission. Like any new applicant, he was asked to submit three drawings, which would allow him to enroll "on probation."

"I tried with 51 little boys, and 19 of us were admitted," he wrote after sending in his application and being accepted. "I go with a large book and a piece of chalk to school every day, like a good little boy." His fellow students were mostly twenty years younger.

In the cartoon he drew accompanying his letter, the other little boys are anything but good or well-behaved. They poke him, somersault, and fly around his easel as tears or perspiration pour down Lear's face. But he looks determined to carry on.

As it turned out, Lear had attended art school for only a short time when attacks of asthma and bronchitis forced him to change his plans. He had to leave London and return to Italy for the winter. From then on he only visited Britain from time to time, spending the next twenty or more years wandering from country to country in search of interesting scenery for his paintings.

6. High Nonsense from Derry Down Derry

For several years a book by a mysterious writer, who called himself Derry Down Derry, circulated around Britain. The author, who said on the front cover that he "loved to see little folks merry," filled each page with fun. The book was an immediate success with children. To the author's astonishment, however, one newspaper critic mistakenly called the book "a reprint of old nursery rhymes." But at the time, only a few of Lear's close friends knew the true author of *A Book of Nonsense*, a slim book containing over a hundred limericks. Here is one of them:

> *There was an Old Man in a tree,*
> *Who was horribly bored by a Bee;*
> > *When they said, 'Does it buzz?'*
> > *He replied, 'Yes, it does!'*
> *'It's a regular brute of a Bee!'*

When Edward Lear decided to claim authorship on the third edition of his book, he

Edward Lear

Book of NONSENSE

was surprised to find, on a visit to Britain, that there were some people who believed that *Edward Lear did not exist!*

This amusing incident, described in one of Lear's letters, took place in a railway carriage when he was on his way to London from Guilford.

Two boys accompanied by two ladies entered the carriage where Lear and an elderly gentleman were seated. The two boys had just been given a copy of the *Book of Nonsense.* "Their laughter infected the whole party," Lear wrote. Noticing the boys' gleeful laughter, the old gentleman asked the ladies if they were aware that the name of the author was fictitious, that it was a disguise for the true author of the book.

"The ladies appeared quite puzzled, as indeed I was," reported Lear.

"I am in a position to know," said the gentleman, "that the true author is a nobleman, none other than Lord Derby. Edward is the Christian name of Lord Derby, and *Lear* is only *Earl* transposed."

"But," said one of the ladies, "the dedication on the book is to the great-grandchildren, grand-nieces, and grand-nephews of the thirteenth Earl of Derby *by Edward Lear.*"

"Merely one more proof that it was the distinguished nobleman who wrote it. A device to confound and confuse us."

"Yet," said one of the ladies, "some friends of mine tell me they met Mr. Lear."

"Until this point I had remained silent," wrote Lear.

"I have reason to know," Lear told the old gentleman, "that Edward Lear, the painter and author, both wrote and illustrated the whole book."

"And *I* have good reason to know, Sir, that you are wholly mistaken. There is no such person as Edward Lear."

"But there is, and I am the man!"

The entire group looked on with astonishment and disbelief. Not until Lear produced his name and address inside his hat label, his monogrammed handkerchief and printed calling cards did the man admit to his error.

"Amazement devoured those benighted individuals and left them gnashing their teeth in trouble and tumult," Lear wrote.

It sometimes did seem that instead of there being *no* Edward Lear there were *two* of them. One was the landscape painter whose friends included nobility and those high up in government, in whose homes he was a frequent visitor. The other was the scrambler of the King's English who turned the days of the week into *Bunday, Toosday,* and *Weddleday,* autumn into *Ortum*—who loved nothing so much as being a little wild and nonsensical. Lear admitted that a part of him never grew up. He once wrote that he was "3 parts crazy—and wholly affectionate."

The number of people to whom he wrote grew and grew. He did not write letters so much as tell stories and hold conversations. Sometimes a letter would begin in a straightforward way, telling about his day: "Rise at six or 6:30—& work a short hour before breakfast at 8. Bkft as slight as possible—2 cups of tea, 2 bits of dry toast, 2 ditto bacon, work till 11—: newspaper. Work again till 2..." and continuing with: "Dine: work again until 7." Then, a typical Lear story begins:

"For a long time I fed on an immense leg of mutton, far, far larger than any leg of mutton I ever saw before or since. But one day I remembered that I had gone to the window to see a Circus Company go by, and attached to that there was an Elephant:—and then the horrid recollection that the circus had returned...but the elephant *never had...!* On the whole," Lear continued, "I do not recommend dead elephant as daily food."

A famous English writer, in trying to define the word *nonsense*, gave this example: "Words—make sense when they relate to things you know. 'Apple' makes sense because we know what an apple is. 'Gropple' does not make sense, since nobody has seen, smelled, heard, tasted or felt a gropple. 'Gropples are fruits which combine the taste of a grape and an apple' seems to make sense, though we would prefer to check...by finding a gropple and eating it." But Lear, the creator of "Calico Pie," "The Owl and the Pussy-cat" and hundreds of rhymes without reason, cared little for definitions. He wrote to please himself—and for the children he liked so much.

Here is Lear's most famous nonsense poem, which has been translated into many languages and, after more than one hundred years, is still loved by young children:

The Owl and the Pussy-cat went to sea
In a beautiful pea-green boat,
They took some honey, and plenty of money,
Wrapped up in a five-pound note.
The Owl looked up to the stars above,
And sang to a small guitar,
'O lovely Pussy! O Pussy, my love,
What a beautiful Pussy you are,
You are,
You are!
What a beautiful Pussy you are!'

Pussy said to the Owl, 'You elegant fowl!
How charmingly sweet you sing!
O let us be married! too long we have tarried:
But what shall we do for a ring?'
They sailed away, for a year and a day,
To the land where the Bong-tree grows
And there in a wood a Piggy-wig stood
With a ring at the end of his nose,
His nose,
His nose,
With a ring at the end of his nose.

'Dear Pig, are you willing to sell for
one shilling
Your ring?' Said the Piggy, 'I will.'
So they took it away, and were married next
day
By the Turkey who lives on the hill.
They dined on mince, and slices of quince,
Which they ate with a runcible spoon;
And hand in hand, on the edge of the sand,
They danced by the light of the moon,
The moon,
The moon,
They danced by the light of the moon.

Runcible, a word Lear made up for the poem above, and later used by Lewis Carroll, has become part of the English language. Though Lear also used the same word to describe his runcible hat, it has come to mean something long and curved, like a pickle fork!

Lear had hundreds and hundreds of names going through his head: Latin names of plants, names of birds and beasts, names of foreign cities and villages, islands, seas, and countries. His letters were sent around the world, as far as New Zealand, where one of his sisters lived. And when he traveled, he spoke other languages: Greek, French, Italian, and some German.

Forced to sit for hours at his drawing table, peck, peck, pecking with a fine metal point, scratching fine dots and lines on a copper plate for his travel prints, was sheer torture for Lear. His body ached. His restless mind rebelled. It was then that he escaped to the place where he was king: the Land of Nonsense. There he was free to create his own language, his own names and places. He invented *Lake Pipple-Popple* on the outskirts of the *City of Tosh, the Hills of the Chankly Bore* on the *Great Gromboolian Plain.* He created a nonsense botany with drawings to match. There was a *Bottlephorkia spoonifolia,* a *Phattfacia stupenda.*

From botany he turned to cookery— creating new rules and recipes, like the one for making *Amblongus Pie.* After an elaborate description, it ends with the following: "Serve up in a clean dish, and throw the whole out of the window as fast as possible."

Lear didn't consider writing limericks or drawing caricatures work. They came naturally and were fun. Nor did he worry about whether or how he'd sell them. But all his life he was haunted by a fear of being in debt—by the memory of his father going to debtor's prison. Whenever his paintings weren't selling, Lear became anxious, working harder and harder. On the other hand, he generously gave away his money to friends and relatives whenever his income improved.

Often, his large landscapes did not sell as

well as he had hoped, even though many, he said, came to "admyer my pigchers." He had more success with his travel books, filled with descriptions and drawings of the lands he had visited. When Lear's book *Journals of a Landscape Painter in Albania* was published in 1851, few foreigners had visited the remote areas of that country, where outsiders were looked on with suspicion and, even, fear.

On his visit to that little-known country, while traveling with his manservant, Giorgio, an Albanian Christian, as his guide and interpreter, Lear set out his materials to sketch an old castle in a wild, mountainous area.

"A shepherd ventured to approach and look at my doings," reported Lear. "He no sooner saw the picture of the castle than he started to shriek out 'Shaitan!' ('Devil')."

It seemed the poor shepherd had never seen an artist copy from life before and saw it as a kind of magic. "Word soon spread to the town where, when they saw me approach, they rushed screaming into their houses, banging their doors shut. Others threw stones." Only after the local bey (a village official) arranged a guard to go with him was the poor, harried artist able to continue to sketch.

This wasn't the only place Lear met with anger and suspicion. Outside Jerusalem, Lear made the mistake of putting Arab tribesmen in his picture, not realizing that making images of Arabs is forbidden by the Islamic religion. When the tribesmen saw what he'd done, they "nipped his ears, pinched his arms, pulled his beard and tore open his pockets, taking all they contained from pounds [British money], to penknives, handkerchiefs and hard-boiled eggs." The eggs were probably for his lunch.

Other times, Lear's unexpected tormentors were a horse, a biting insect, or both, as in Greece. On a single trip into the mountains Lear returned battered and sore from a fall from his horse, a bite from a scorpion, and a fever from sunstroke.

None of this stopped him from going, day after day, in search of new scenery. He returned from each new trip with hundreds of sketches. No one would suspect from the serene-looking landscapes he drew, the hardship and effort they involved. This wild, strange world Lear visited as a wandering artist reappeared, in a way, in his tales for children, tales of places where anything could happen.

View of Ceriana, 1870 by Edward Lear

The Adopty Duncle

C. 1865

Self portrait

The Jumblies

Enkoopia Chickabiddia

7. Oh, What Nonsense, Mr. Lear

Tigulillia Terribilis

It had been twenty-five years since Lear had published his first book for children—not that he had stopped writing for them. His friends among children numbered in the hundreds—he was their *adopty duncle.*

One friend was Margaret Terry, with whom he took walks in the forest, kicking chestnut burrs as they went, calling them *yonghy-bonghy-bos.* They were guests at the same hotel. Every day, a letter of his new nonsense alphabet was set at the lunch plate of Margaret and her brother, Arthur, drawn in pen and ink and tinted with watercolors. It started with *A*, with a drawing of *the Absolutely Abstemious Ass,* and finished with *Z* and *the Zigzag Zealous Zebra.* For his friend Evelyn Baring's son, who was having difficulty learning his colors, Lear painted a complete little book called *Lear's Coloured Bird Book for Children.* Birds were still a favorite subject of his, many looking like people—or did the people look like birds? No matter. The drawings were funny and appealing.

In the new book, published in 1871, called *Nonsense, Songs, Stories, Botany and Alphabets*, he introduced the Jumblies, who went to sea in a sieve.

In a Sieve they went to sea:
In spite of all their friends could say,
On a winter's morn, on a stormy day,
In a Sieve they went to sea!

We are told that "their heads are green and their hands are blue...that they sail in the Sieve to the Western Sea...to a land all covered with trees."

Just a year later his third book, *More Nonsense, Pictures, Rhymes, Botany, Etc.*, containing one hundred new limericks, appeared in print. From that day forward Lear was forever king of limerick makers. There seemed no limit to the invented creatures coming from his pen. Five years later a fourth book, *Laughable Lyrics*, introduced "The Dong with the Luminous Nose," "The Popples," and "Mr. & Mrs. Discobbolos."

This highly talented artist, who was both ambitious and modest, some years earlier had written a verse he called a "self-portrait." It begins with the words he overheard one day: "How pleasant to know Mr. Lear." Starting with the same words, he added:

Who has written such volumes of stuff!
Some think him ill-tempered and queer,
    But a few think him pleasant enough.
His mind is concrete and fastidious,
    His nose is remarkably big;
His visage is more or less hideous,
    His beard it resembles a wig...etc.

With all its nonsense and humor, the portrait in many ways was correct. Counting all his letters and travel and nonsense books, he *had* written a volume of stuff, never imagining his limericks and poems would be more famous than his landscape paintings, books on travel, or even his acclaimed animal prints. Some years after his death, one of his biographers wrote that early editions of his nonsense books "are not to be found, most of them having been used up or eaten up by the children for whom they were written."

In 1871, after long years of living the life of a wandering landscape painter, Lear built himself a house in San Remo, Italy, overlooking the Mediterranean Sea. At fifty-nine, Lear had, at last, a permanent home of his own. A striped kitten became part of the household, a kitten with "no end of tale," having somehow lost the tip of it. The kitten, given the name of Foss, became as much a part of the household as Giorgio. He was the model for dozens of sketches of cats with dash and personality: prancing, dancing, playful felines that mostly existed in the imagination of his master.

Foss was, alas, a poor traveler and had to be left at the villa in the care of servants or a friend when his master took one of his long trips abroad. But these became fewer and fewer as time went on.

Traveling had become more and more difficult as Lear grew older. Though never too fond of sea voyages, especially in the winter when the sea was rough, he had crossed the Mediterranean, Adriatic, and North seas many times. Airplane travel did not yet exist, so trips across oceans could only be made by ship. Overland, he had gone on foot, horseback, or camelback. In the mountains of Lebanon, the deserts of Egypt, the hills of the Holy Land, there were few or no roads.

Even as a young man, the trips had been physically exhausting for him. Now his restlessness was gone. Sister Ann had died several years earlier in England, and he had been there to give her a flower and hold her hand each day until the end. There were few reasons for returning to England anymore. His friends, busy with their families and careers or too old to want visitors, no longer welcomed him as before.

For three years Lear gave up painting almost entirely to sketch and write stories for children. But he was once again faced with the problem of earning money. When a letter arrived from India one day, he was tempted to take a last, long journey, this time to paint the landscapes of India, which was ruled at the time by Great Britain.

An invitation had come from an old friend, who had been made the viceroy of India, to spend a year or more traveling as his guest in this vast Asian country. For almost a year, Lear was undecided about whether to go, but finally the idea of seeing India and returning with a large number of new landscapes proved to be too tempting. With many regrets about leaving his pleasant home in San Remo, Lear and faithful Giorgio set out for the difficult journey.

There was an Old Man of Calcutta,
Who perpetually ate bread and butter;
    Till a great bit of muffin,
        On which he was stuffing,
Choked that horrid old man of Calcutta.

8. India and "The Akond of Swat"

"Extreme beauty of Bombay Harbour!... wonderful variety of life and dress here," wrote Lear when he arrived in India. Lear had not lost his artist's eye for beauty even after the long and tiring trip. As soon as he was unpacked, he left Giorgio to arrange their living quarters and set off to sketch.

For over a year Lear crisscrossed the huge country, returning with over five hundred drawings, large and small, besides nine small sketchbooks and four journals. Even after working under the most unpleasant conditions—heat, buzzing insects, sudden storms, glaring sun—the beauty of India's landscapes kept him going day after day. Its temples, its "parrot-coloured people and dress," as he described it, amazed and inspired him.

"I... began a regular street scene and worked my eyes nearly out of my head. Nothing can give the least idea of the splendour of colour here: the world seems turned into a rainbow!" wrote Lear.

Lrd. Northbrook

Giorgno Kokali

No other landscape painter had attempted to record so much of India in so short a time as had Edward Lear.

Lear was a frequent guest of British families stationed in India. His long workday often ended entertaining his British host and family at the dinner table, as he had done years ago at Knowsley. He was always pleased on these occasions when the children recognized him as the man who had written *A Book of Nonsense*. He not only recited his limericks for them but would sit at the piano and sing the songs he'd written for his poems. He had set "The Owl and the Pussy-cat" to music and often sang it lustily for the hostess's children.

In his diary he recorded that he was deeply touched when an incident, described below, occurred in an Anglo-Indian hotel where he was staying.

Before dinner, while drawing birds for the landlord's little daughter, "another little girl, just as I was drawing an owl, called out, 'O please draw a pussy-cat too! because you know they went to sea in a boat, with plenty of honey and money wrapped up in a £5 note!' On enquiry I found that she and all her schoolmates had been taught that remarkable poem!"

The Indian trip inspired two new poems for his next book, *Laughable Lyrics:* "The Cummerbund" and "The Akond of Swat," which begins:

Who, or why or which or what, *Is the*
                    Akond of SWAT?
Is he tall or short, or dark or fair?
Does he sit on a stool or a sofa or chair,...
                    or SQUAT?
                    The Akond of Swat?
  Is he wise or foolish, young or old?
Does he drink his soup and his coffee cold,
                    or HOT,
                    The Akond of Swat?
Does he sing or whistle, jabber or talk,
And when riding abroad does he gallop
                    or TROT,
                    The Akond of Swat?

The poem continues, rhyming the name *Swat* with pot, what, cot, dot, blot, plot, shot, garotte, jot, and more.

Lear drew a portrait of himself and Giorgio riding an elephant with the Akond of Swat underneath. No one, including the author, seemed to know who or which or why or what...is the Akond of Swat, for in the cartoon he appears more like a funny old bird than a man.

When Giorgio became very ill with dysentery, Lear cut short his trip to India and returned to Italy. It was Lear's last long journey. The wanderer wanted nothing so much as the peace and quiet of his home and studio in San Remo. He hoped to finish one more book of travel, this one on India, and to complete a huge landscape—fifteen feet long by nine feet high. The painting was so large that it could only be hung inside a grand manor house or a museum. To the end, Edward Lear hoped to be recognized as one of Britain's great landscape painters.

The Akkond
of Swat

67

During Lear's absence from Italy, the land in front of his villa had been sold and a large hotel was about to be built there. The new hotel would block his view of the sea and, worst of all, would shut out the north light he depended on in order to paint. His eyesight was getting worse with each passing year. He had no choice but to move.

In the summer of 1881, Lear, Foss, Giorgio, and Giorgio's two sons, who also had come to work for Lear, moved into the new villa. It was built exactly like the first one, so Foss would feel at home and have a sunny corner to sleep in. Measured by a cat's lifetime, Foss was now an old cat, over thirteen years old. Instead of the dancing, prancing pet he had drawn years ago, Lear now drew him round and whiskered, walking behind a bearded man (himself) with toothpick legs.

Edward Lear.
aet 73.½

His cat Foss,
aet 16.

O my agèd Uncle Arly!
Sitting on a heap of Barley
    Thro' the silent hours
..ose beside a leafy thicket
.. his nose there was a
.. his hat a Railew
    (But his shoes
        were far too
            Tight.

Giorgio, his good servant and companion of twenty-seven years, died two years later, leaving his sons to care for his grieving employer. Calling him "my poor dear George," Lear wrote just after he died, "I wish I could think that I merited such a friend." Gentle Giorgio had traveled the world with Lear, cheerfully accepting the bad with the good.

Four years later Foss died and was given a proper burial and headstone in the garden of the new house. "All those who have known my life will understand that I grieve over this loss," wrote Lear. Now he felt truly alone!

At the beginning of the year 1888, just three months after the loss of his beloved cat, Lear died. He had nearly completed his travel book on India and the huge oil painting. Scribbled on the yellow pages of a kind of notebook were parts of unfinished poems and a rough version of "My Aged Uncle Arly." One of his unfinished fragments was a sequel to "The Owl and the Pussy-cat." It was called "The Children of the Owl and the Pussy-cat," and started this way:

Our mother was the Pussy-cat, our father
was the Owl,
And so we're partly little beasts and partly
little fowl,
The brothers of our family have feathers
and they hoot,
While all the sisters dress in fur and have long
tails to boot.
We all believe that little mice,
For food are singularly nice.
but what of that?

The poem continued for several more stanzas, with spaces left for unfinished lines.

Sometimes Lear used to wonder how he came to reach the ripe old age of seventy-six. With all his aches and pains, he had outlived his brothers and sisters. To the very end, for Edward Lear, life remained most puzzling and queer.

And, to end this story as he once ended his letter:

No more my pen: no more my ink:
No more my rhyme is clear.
So I shall leave off here I think—
Yours ever,
Edward Lear

I am grown horribly fat from want of exercise —like this—

BIBLIOGRAPHY

Byrom, Thomas. *Nonsense and Wonder: The Poems and Cartoons of Edward Lear.* New York: E. P. Dutton, 1977.

Davidson, Angus. *Edward Lear: Landscape Painter and Nonsense Poet.* London: John Murray, Publisher, 1938.

Hark, Ina. *Edward Lear.* Boston: Twayne Publishers, 1982.

Jackson, Holbrook. *The Complete Nonsense of Edward Lear.* Chicago: Dover Publications, 1951.

Kelen, Emery. *Mr. Nonsense: A Life of Edward Lear.* Nashville: Thomas Nelson, 1973.

Lear, Edward. *Indian Journals.* Edited by Ray Murphy. London: Jarrolds Publishers, 1953.

Lehmann, John. *Edward Lear & His World.* New York: Charles Scribner's Sons, Thames & Hudson, 1977.

Noakes, Vivien. *Edward Lear: The Life of a Wanderer.* London: Collins, 1968.

————. *Edward Lear: Selected Letters.* Oxford: Clarendon Press, 1988.

————. *Edward Lear, 1812 to 1888.* New York: Harry Abrams, 1986.

Rakel, Robert E., M.D. *Epilepsy and Personality: Textbook of Family Practice.* Philadelphia: W. B. Saunders, 1984.

Richardson, Joanna. *Edward Lear: Writers and Their Works.* London: Longman Green, 1965.

Strachey, Constance. *Letters of Edward Lear.* London: T. Fisher Unwin, 1907.

————. *Later Letters of Edward Lear.* London: T. Fisher Unwin, 1911.

Temkin, Owsei. *The Falling Sickness: The History of Epilepsy.* Baltimore: Johns Hopkins Press, 1945.

ACKNOWLEDGMENTS

To my friends, Rosalie Feder and Cynthia Davies, as well as to my husband, all of whom gave me valuable suggestions and criticism, my thanks. I am also indebted to Anthony Burgess for his clear definition of the word *nonsense* quoted from his article titled "Let's Talk Nonsense."

To the staff of the Children's Literature Center of the Library of Congress for the use of their comfortable chairs, desk, their books and printouts, my warm appreciation once again.

No book would reach its final printed, polished state without the help of its editor, so to Marcia Marshall for midwifing once again... thank you.